KU-103-589

The big game

This book belongs to

____

Written by Stephen Barnett
Illustrated by Rosie Brooks

Contents

About this book

Stories for the confident reader, bringing with them new ideas and concepts that will make learning to read an enjoyment.

The big game

This was it! The final soccer game of the year was about to begin! Our soccer team, the Tigers have played hard all year. We have won seven games and lost just two. Today is the grand final game between the Tigers and the Bears.

'Gather around, team,' the coach called out. 'Well, you have all played really well this year and now you have a chance to win the cup. So, go out, play well and win the cup. Good luck!' he said.

We lined up behind Kerry, our captain and ran on to the pitch. We shook hands with the players from the Bears and wished them good luck. I was feeling a bit nervous. I looked over to my parents and sister who were standing on the sideline. They gave me a big wave.

'Okay,' said the referee to both the captains. 'Let's toss the coin to see which way you will play in the first half.' Kerry won the toss and decided that we would play into the wind for the first half. The referee blew his whistle and the game began!

In the first few minutes there were long kicks up and down the field. Then the game got faster and I had more work to do. I was trying to stop the players from the Bears team from kicking the ball to our goal.

Our midfield players and the strikers at the front worked hard to take the ball forward and try to score. Nina was the best of our players at the front.

'Phweet!' That was the whistle for half-time. The score was 0-0. We ran off the field, grabbed bottles of water and sat down in front of the coach.

'Team, you are all playing a great game out there. Our defence is holding up well and the forwards are trying hard to score. Be patient and I'm sure it will happen,' he said.

In the second half, the Bears ran towards our goal post. I ran forward and tried to take the ball away from their player. But before I got to him he kicked the ball across the field towards the goal. The ball sailed into the middle of the pitch right in front of our goal! Their striker kicked it hard into the net. Oh no! They had scored one goal!

We took up our positions for the kick-off. In a kick-off, a player kicks the ball from a centre spot. Only ten minutes were left and we needed to score. A single goal was enough to draw the game. Our families and friends began to cheer for us.

With just one minute to go before the end of the game, their goalkeeper kicked a long ball down field. I ran forward to stop it. 'It's now or never!' I thought as I got the ball at my feet. I ran on towards the Bears' goal. I dribbled the ball around one of the Bears, and then around another of their players.

Nina was in position in front of their goal. I gave a big kick to the ball, sending it to Nina. For a moment it looked as if I had hit the ball too hard but she got her boot to it and trapped it. Then she turned and in a one movement hooked the ball into the corner of the goal. I watched as the goalkeeper jumped to save the shot but Nina's kick was too strong. One goal each!

Then the final whistle went and we all ran over to congratulate Nina. I also got a few pats on the back for the kick that I had made.

As the result was a draw, the trophy was presented to the captains of both the teams. Maybe, next year the Tigers will play a little better!

The time travellers

'Set the dial for last Thursday,' Simon called out.
'Set it about four o'clock in the afternoon.'
'It is set at four o' clock,' his sister Karina answered. 'Any particular place you want to start looking?'
'Let's start with the living-room. I'm sure that's where I left it.'
'You're always losing things! Lucky we have got the Time Machine.'

Simon jumped down from the chair on which he was standing to make a final check of the wings of the Time Machine.
'Ready?' Karina looked in Simon's direction as he strapped himself into his seat.
'All okay. Fire it up!'

Karina pushed the big red button by the steering wheel and waited. For a few seconds nothing happened. And then, there came a low drumming sound which became louder and louder. On the screen in front of Karina, colours danced and there was a mass of numbers. 'Time and date selected!' she called to her brother. 'We are off!'

There was a flash of blue light from the top of the Time Machine and the craft shook faster and faster. Karina and Simon held on to the edges of their seats as the machine shot back and forth across the floor, its wheels whirring. Then suddenly everything went white. There was total silence.

A few days back Simon had found the old book called 'Time in Your Hands' at the back of the bookshelf in the school library. To his surprise he discovered that it was a guide-book on travelling through time!

The book described how (if you could only go fast enough) you could squeeze time and be pushed forward. Simon imagined that this was a bit like what happened when he squeezed the middle of the toothpaste tube and the toothpaste squeezed out. 'Go fast enough and you could squeeze time so much that you could even go backwards in time,' the book said.

Simon had read the book with Karina. They had stared for hours at the drawings and diagrams of machines in which they might travel through time. Would it really work?

After building one of the machines in the book, they were able to make short trips backwards and forwards in time. The trip they were on now was to take them to last Thursday. It was made to find Simon's favourite sweatshirt which he had lost.

Now they could see where they were. They were in the living room and luckily there was no one else to be surprised at their magical arrival. They could hear their mother in the kitchen singing along to a song on the radio while she was getting the evening meal ready.

'Is that you, Karina?' their mother called out. 'Yes, mum, me and Simon.' Karina hurriedly threw a cover over the Time Machine just as their mother walked in.

'I thought that you both had gone outside to play.'
'Oh, it was starting to rain. So we decided to play inside and make a tent,' said Karina pointing to the cover.
'Well, if it's raining then you'd better bring your sweatshirt in, Simon. You have left it outside on the grass.'
Karina looked at Simon.

'Sure, mum, I'll get it now. By the way, I think I can guess what we will have for dinner – fish!'
'Now, how did you know that?' asked their mother. A good guess!'
Simon winked at Karina.

Their mother went back to the kitchen. Karina quickly took off the cover from the Time Machine as her brother returned with his sweatshirt. 'Come on, let's head back!' said Simon to his sister

New words

belt

coach

congratulate

defence

direction

dribble

forward

gather

goalkeeper

grand

half-time

luckily

midfield

nervous

pitch

position

referee

select

soccer

striker

sweatshirt

trophy

What did you learn?

The big game

What were the names of the teams?

What was the name of the captain of the Tigers?

What was the score at the end of the match?

The time travellers

What were the names of the children?

What were they looking for?

Where in the house did the Time Machine land?